Holly Reid is a 25-year-old Optometrist from a small rural village in County Antrim, Northern Ireland. She studied at Cardiff University before returning home to begin her career. She lives with her mum, dad, and two sisters, along with their much-loved family pet, Alfie, an 11-year-old West Highland Terrier. This is her debut book inspired by Alfie's adventures over the years!

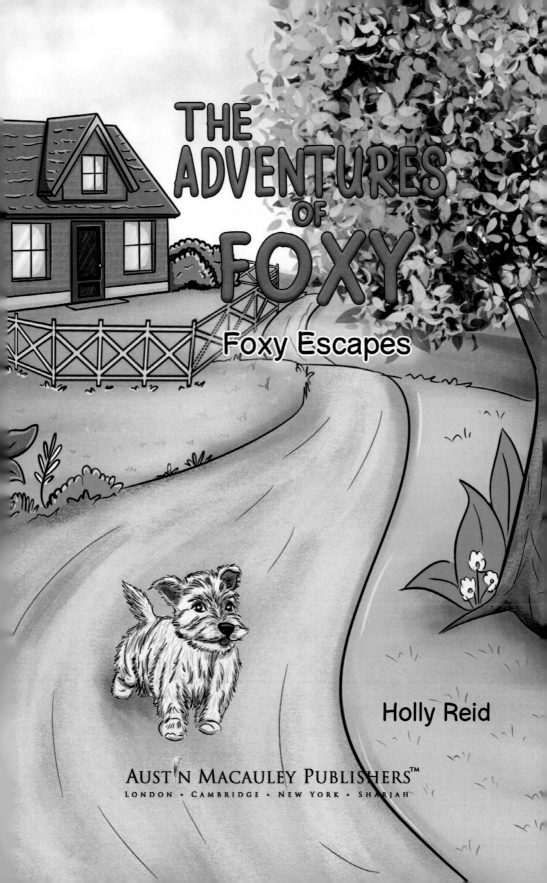

THE ADVENTURES OF FOXY

Foxy Escapes

Holly Reid

AUSTIN MACAULEY PUBLISHERS™
LONDON • CAMBRIDGE • NEW YORK • SHARJAH

A CIP catalogue record for this title is available from the British Library.

ISBN 9781398448100 (Paperback)
ISBN 9781398448117 (ePub e-book)

www.austinmacauley.com

First Published 2022
Austin Macauley Publishers Ltd®
1 Canada Square
Canary Wharf
London
E14 5AA

For my wee dog Alfie, my inspiration and best friend always xx

A huge thanks to my family for always encouraging me to chase my dreams and to those at Austin Macauley Publishers for their guidance and continued support.

I have this dog called Foxy,
He looks nothing like a fox.
He chases things around
the garden,
And barks an awful lot.

One morning
eating breakfast,
Foxy was nowhere
to be found.
Mummy called out "Foxy!"
But he didn't make
a sound.

We started looking
round the house,
Running up and
down the stairs.

He likes to sleep in
our beds at night,
But when we looked,
he wasn't there.

He wasn't hiding behind
the couch,
Or sitting at the
front door.

He didn't run into
the kitchen,
To lick our toast crumbs
off the floor.

We grabbed our coats,
put on shoes,
And ran to
look outside.

I knew Foxy would be
hard to find,
With so many more
places to hide.

My sister
started shouting,
"Foxy come and
get some food!"

He didn't run up
to the door,
Maybe he just
wasn't in the mood.

Daddy and I
started looking,
Where Foxy likes to play,
We went to all his
favourite spots,
Looking for clues
along the way.

I went to check the
flowers first,
He likes to drink water
from their pots.
But I knew he hadn't
been there,
When I saw there was
still lots.

Mummy was looking
through the shed,
Where daddy keeps
his tools.

I was sure Foxy wouldn't
be there,
He knows it's against
the rules!

Daddy went through the
bushes next,
Where Foxy likes
to play,

With hedgehogs, frogs
and next door's dog,
He could play in there
all day!

Suddenly I spotted,
Our fence had quite
a hole.

It was big enough
for Foxy,
He must have gone out
for a stroll!

We found him wandering
up the lane,
I ran and held
him tight.

I told him to never run
away again,
As he'd given me
a fright!

I didn't want to worry,
When Foxy went
out to play,

But I knew it
wasn't fair,
To keep him inside
all day.

Daddy said he would
fill the hole,
And mend the
broken wood.

Foxy shouldn't get
out again,
Let's hope this time,
for good!

THE END